This Little Tiger
book belongs to:

_____

_____

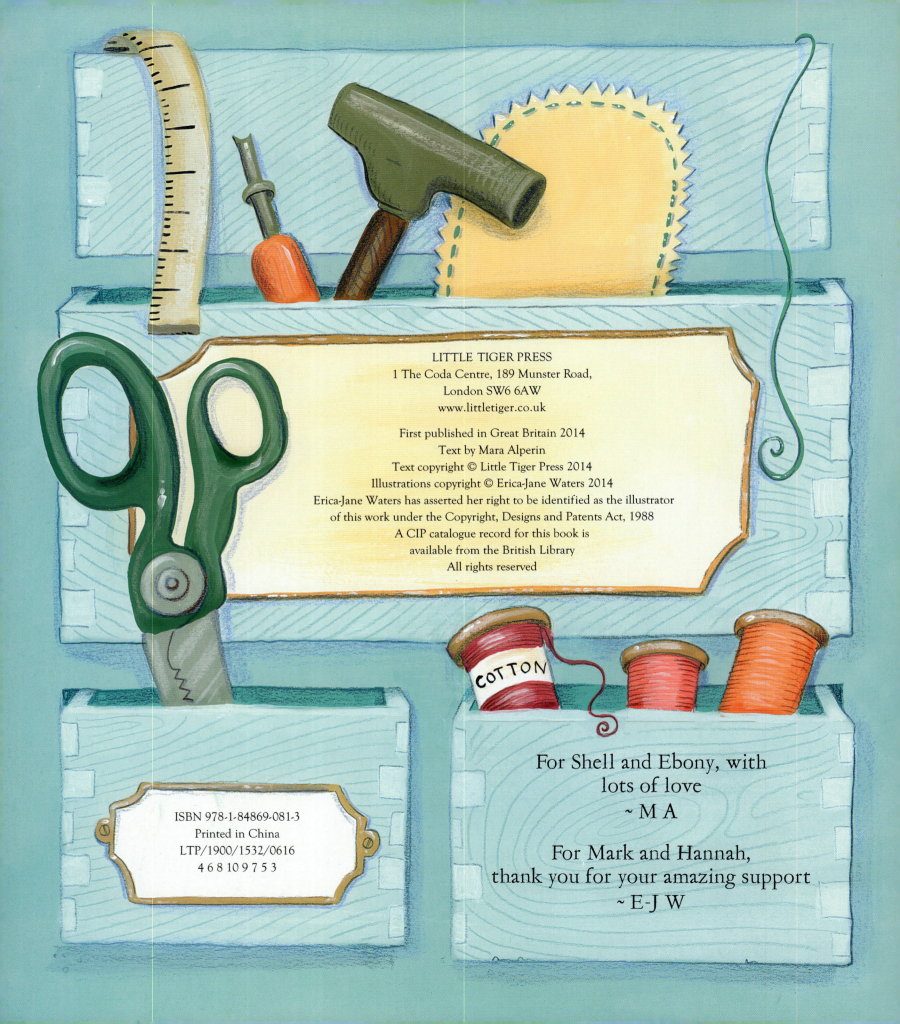

LITTLE TIGER PRESS
1 The Coda Centre, 189 Munster Road,
London SW6 6AW
www.littletiger.co.uk

First published in Great Britain 2014
Text by Mara Alperin
Text copyright © Little Tiger Press 2014
Illustrations copyright © Erica-Jane Waters 2014
Erica-Jane Waters has asserted her right to be identified as the illustrator
of this work under the Copyright, Designs and Patents Act, 1988
A CIP catalogue record for this book is
available from the British Library

ISBN 978-1-84869-081-3
Printed in China
LTP/1900/1532/0616
4 6 8 10 9 7 5 3

For Shell and Ebony, with
lots of love
~ M A

For Mark and Hannah,
thank you for your amazing support
~ E-J W

The Elves and the Shoemaker

Mara Alperin

Illustrated by
Erica-Jane Waters

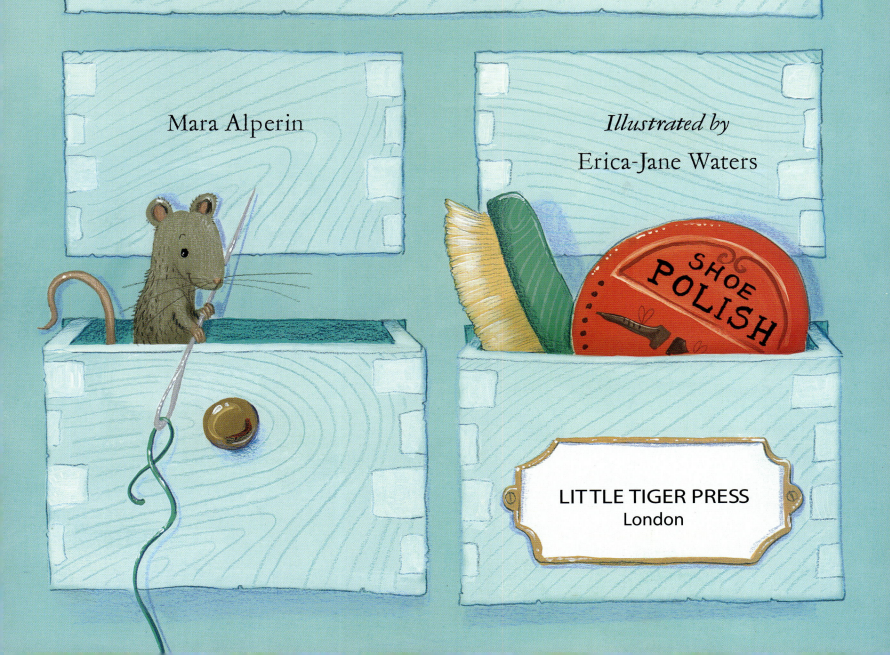

LITTLE TIGER PRESS
London

In an old and shabby shoe shop,
there lived a cobbler, Stan,
and his wife, Jan.

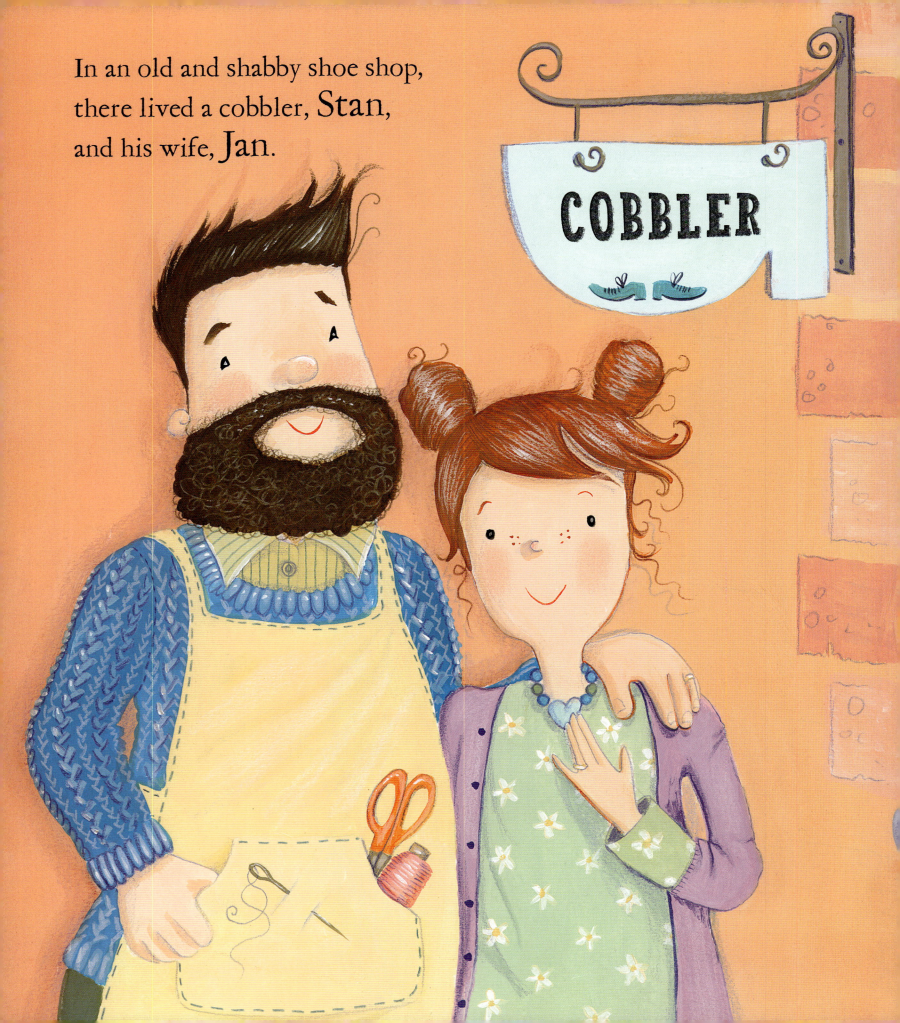

Though they were poor, they were very happy,
for they loved to make shoes . . .
Shoes for **walking** and shoes for **jumping**, shoes for **skipping**...

and **best** of all,
shoes for
dancing!

Every day, Stan and Jan
worked hard making
shoes for their
little shop . . .

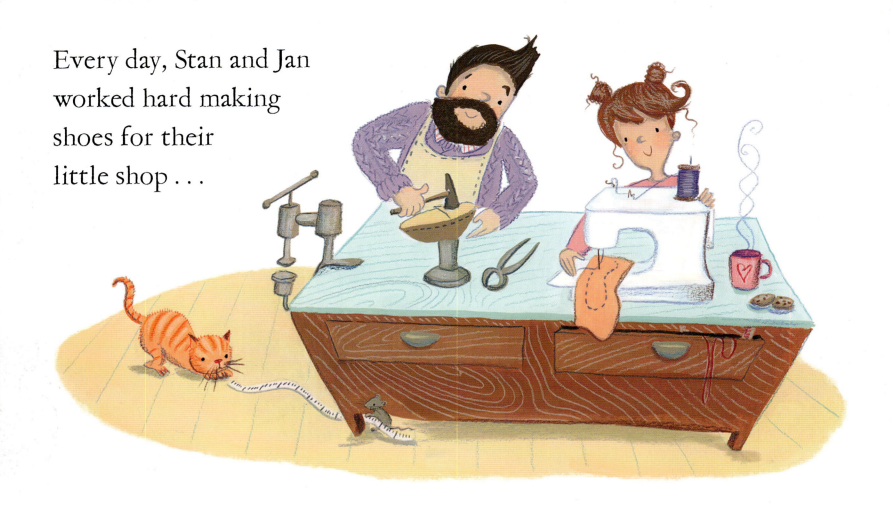

and every evening, they slipped on
their favourite dancing shoes and
waltzed the night away.

The villagers loved to watch them dance,
and before long, people young and old **whirled**
and **twirled** through the door to join in.

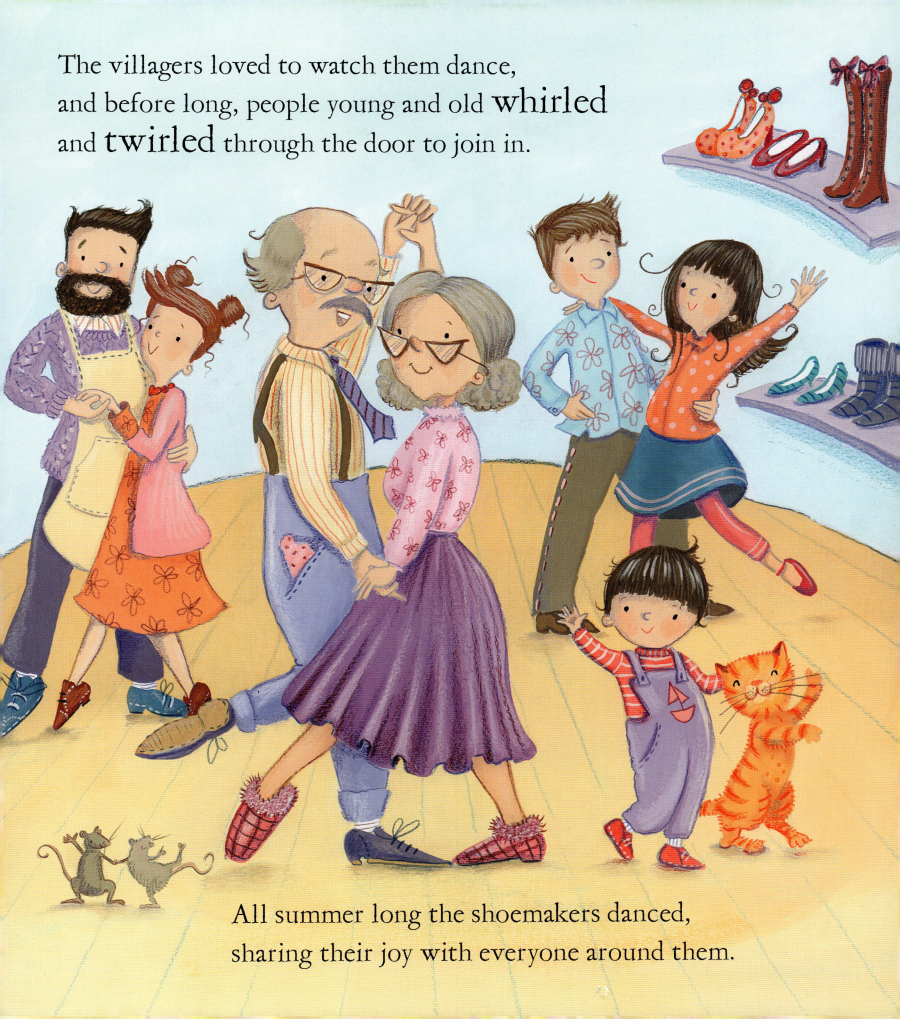

All summer long the shoemakers danced,
sharing their joy with everyone around them.

But soon the bitter winter came.

And as the weeks passed, fewer and fewer customers stopped to buy shoes.

"Whatever will we do?" worried Stan. "Soon we will have no money left and no more firewood!"

The shop grew quieter . . .   and quieter . . .

That night, Stan and Jan huddled by the tiny fire, their fingers too cold to sew and their feet too frozen to dance.

"Let's g-g-go to b-b-bed," Jan chattered. "Perhaps we'll think of something in the morning."

But in the morning they awoke to find the most
magnificent pair of shoes.
"Leaping laces! Who made these?"
marvelled Stan.

Before they could start
to wonder . . .

the shop door opened, and in marched their
first customer in weeks.

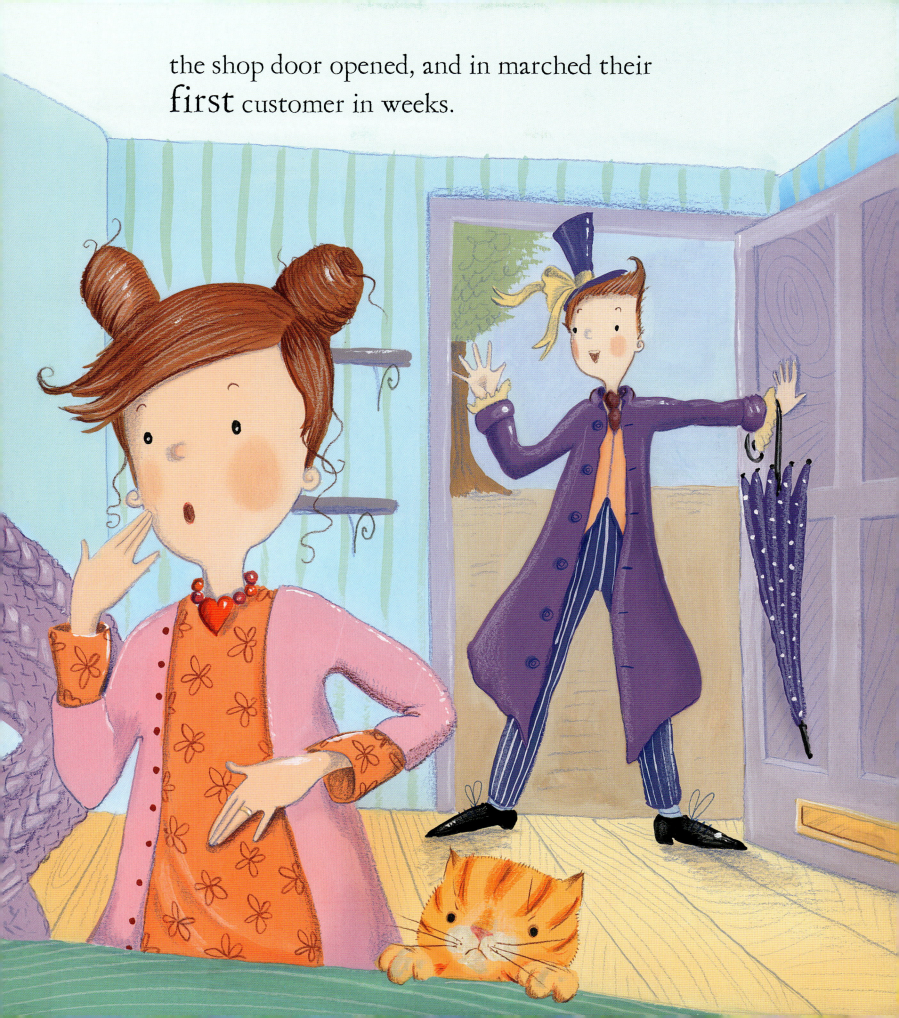

"Good day!" cried the customer. "My name is Sir Flumby. I spied these **splendid** shoes in the window and I simply **must** have them!"

The shoes fitted **perfectly**.

So, Sir Flumby paid Stan a handful of gold pieces, and skipped away merrily in his new shoes.

Delighted, Stan went to the market to buy some supper and firewood.

And that night, the shoemaker and his wife danced with joy once more!

The next morning they found, to their amazement, **three** new pairs of shoes even more **stunning** than the last!

Stan and Jan could not believe their eyes! But just then . . .

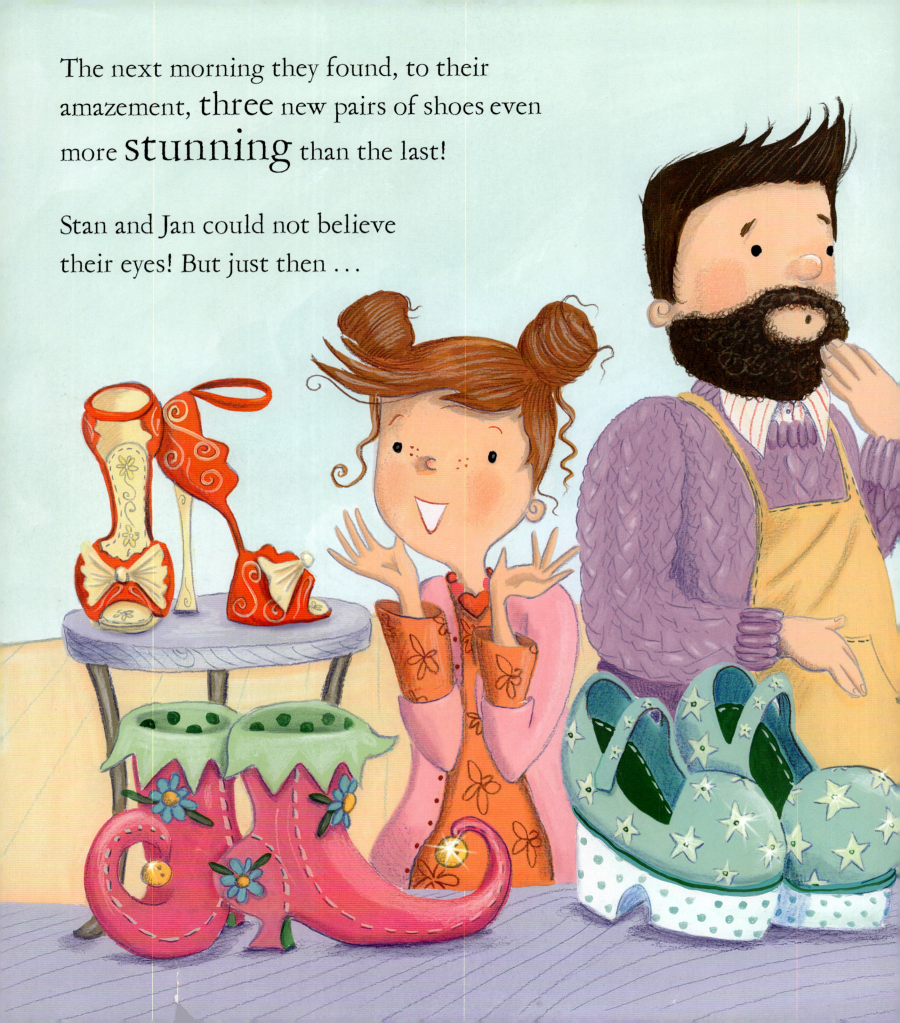

"Greetings, Shoemakers!
I am Sir Flipsy-Flopsy, and
I have heard tales of your
marvellous shoes."

"Why, they are even more
fabulous than I imagined,"
he bellowed. "I shall buy
them **all** – one pair for
me, and the others for my
horse, Toby."

So, Sir Flipsy-Flopsy
filled the shoemakers'
pockets with gold coins,
and **galloped** off.

From then on, there were shiny new shoes every morning. Soon the shop was warm and cosy and bustling with customers day after day.

One day, Jan said, "We still don't know who is helping us. I wish we could thank them!"

Then Stan had a wonderful idea. "Why don't we stay up and find out?"

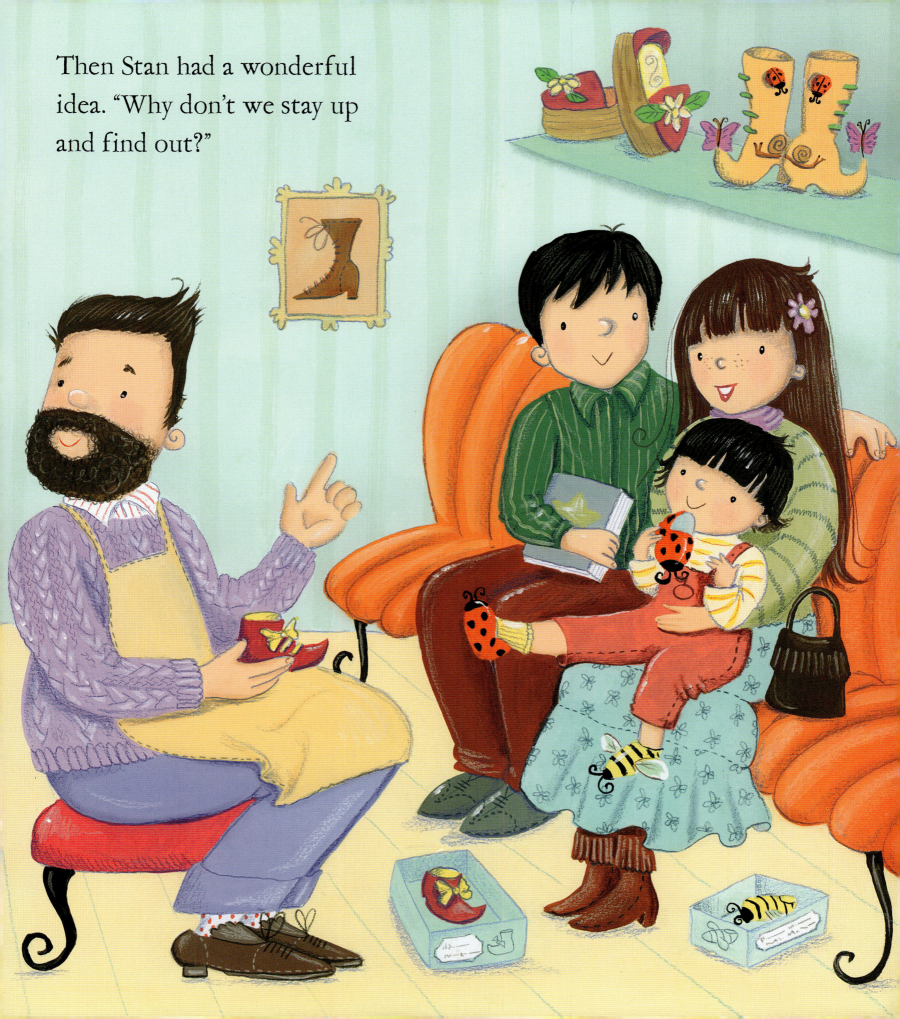

So that night, Jan and Stan hid behind the curtains. They waited, and **waited**, and **waited** …

until, as the clock struck **midnight** …

three tiny elves slipped in through the keyhole …

and t i p t o e d across the room!

The elves set to work with a stitch, stitch, stitch, and a rap-a-tap-tap. And as they worked, they sang:

We love jumping, leaping, prancing,
We were sad when you stopped dancing.
So in we creep while you are dreaming,
Making new shoes, bright and gleaming!

All night the elves sewed, until the sun began to rise.

And then quickly, quietly, they popped back through the keyhole.

Stan and Jan were so surprised by what they'd seen.

"What delightful little elves," Stan whispered. "We must repay their kindness."

"Let's make them their own little dancing shoes," said Jan. "And some dancing clothes, too."

So, the next morning, that's just what they did. Jan knitted tiny jumpers, using tiny pins . . .

then sewed on tiny apple pips for decoration.

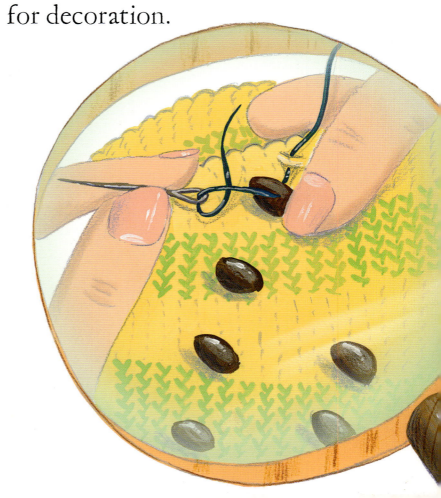

Stan crafted tiny shoes
from dandelion leaves . . .

then stitched them
with daisy stem laces.

And together they made little pointy hats,
finished with the tiniest pom-poms.

At midnight, Stan left the tiny parcel on the workbench, just before the three little elves crept inside.

For our very special helpers, may you dance the night away. With love, Jan & Stan xx

When the elves saw their new clothes, they were **overjoyed!**

They giggled and wiggled,
and danced all night in
the moonlight.

But as the stars faded,
the three tiny elves
t i p t o e d away, and
vanished
into the night.

That was the last the shoemakers ever saw of the elves. But their kindness was never forgotten, and Stan and Jan danced **every** night with their friends just in case the elves ever returned.

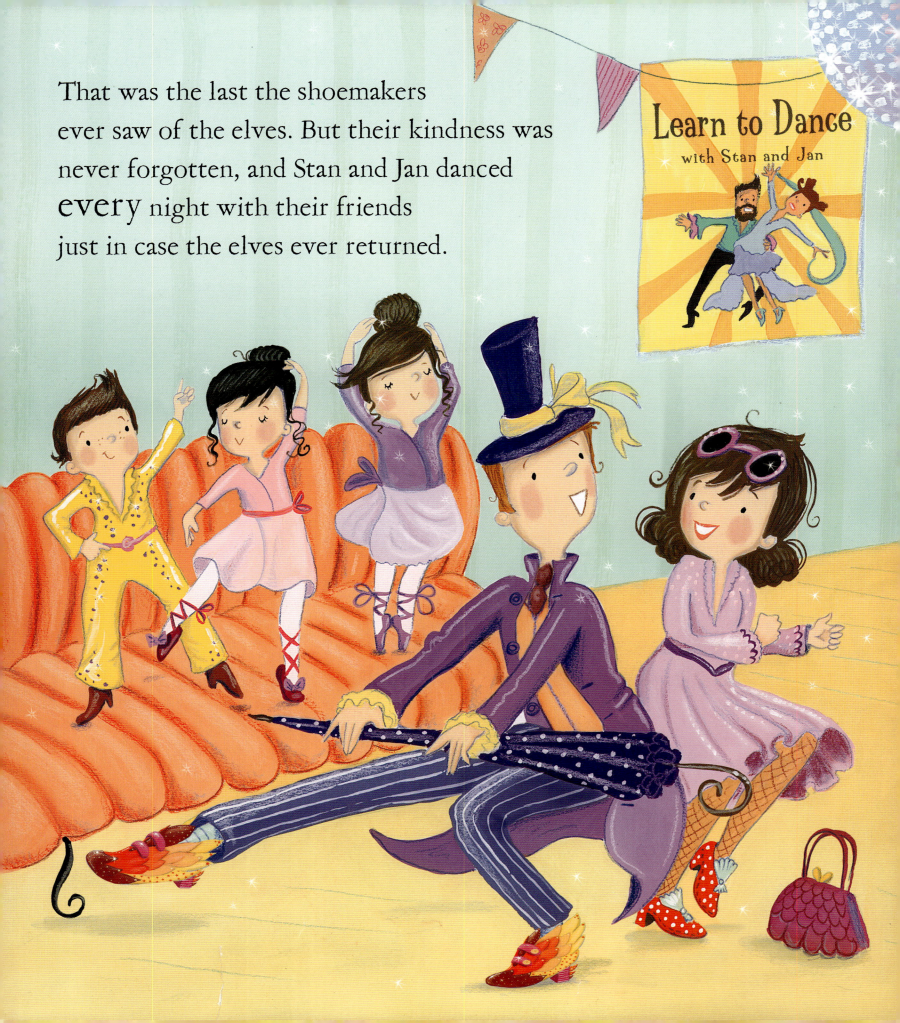

Learn to Dance
with Stan and Jan

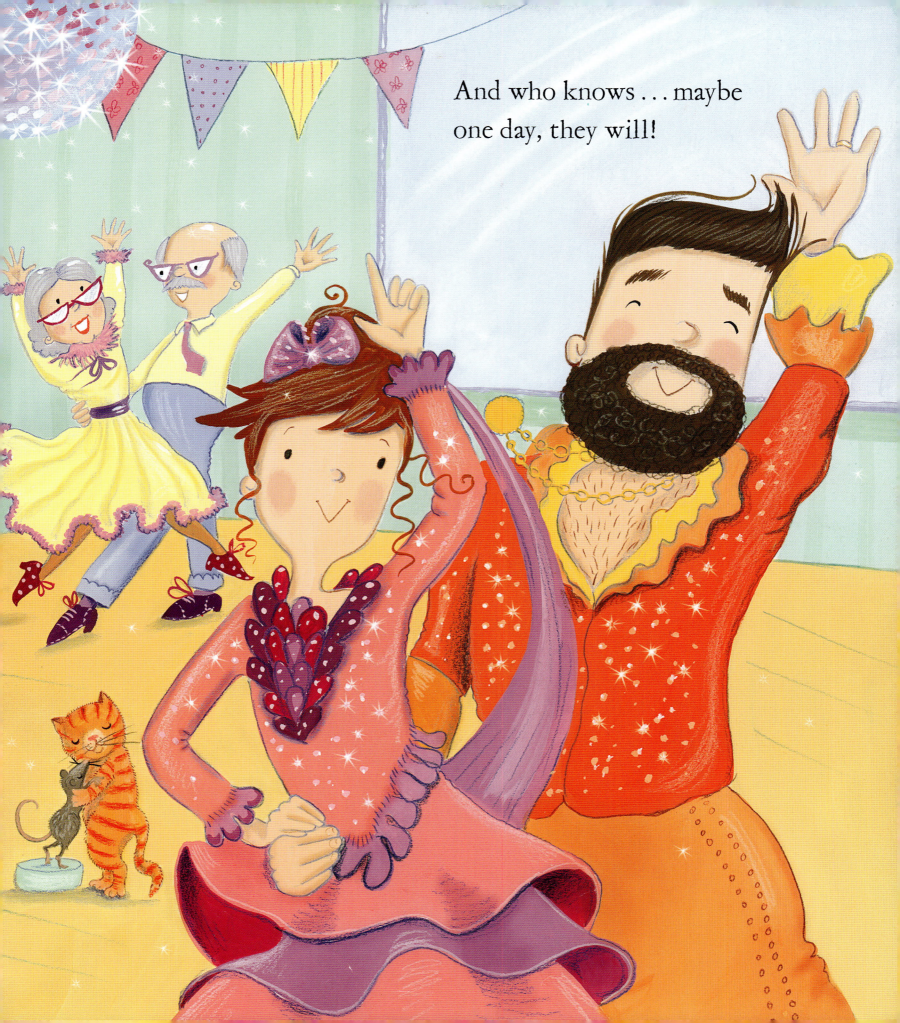

And who knows . . . maybe one day, they will!

My First Fairy Tales

are familiar, fun and friendly stories – with a marvellously modern twist!

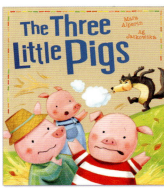

The Three Little Pigs
Mara Alperin
Ag Jatkowska

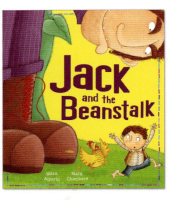

Jack and the Beanstalk
Mara Alperin
Mark Chambers

Mara Alperin · Loretta Schauer
Rumpelstiltskin

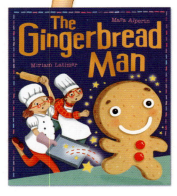

The Gingerbread Man
Mara Alperin
Miriam Latimer

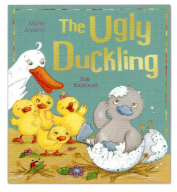

Mara Alperin
The Ugly Duckling
Sue Eastland

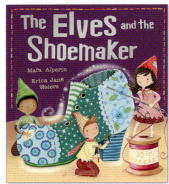

The Elves and the Shoemaker
Mara Alperin
Erica Jane Waters

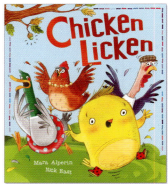

Chicken Licken
Mara Alperin
Nick East

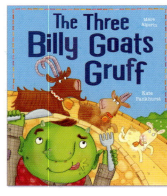

The Three Billy Goats Gruff
Mara Alperin
Kate Pankhurst

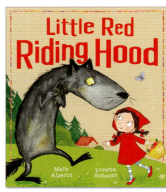

Little Red Riding Hood
Mara Alperin
Loretta Schauer

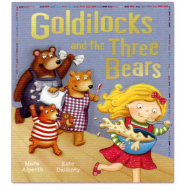

Goldilocks and the Three Bears
Mara Alperin
Kate Daubney